Henry the Reading Dog

written by Diana Kotula Reich

AuthorHouse™
1663 Liberty Drive
Bloomington, IN 47403
www.authorhouse.com
Phone: 833-262-8899

Because of the dynamic nature of the Internet, any web addresses or links contained in this book may have changed
since publication and may no longer be valid. The views expressed in this work are solely those of the author and do
not necessarily reflect the views of the publisher, and the publisher hereby disclaims any responsibility for them.

Any people depicted in stock imagery provided by Getty Images are models,
and such images are being used for illustrative purposes only.
Certain stock imagery © Getty Images.

This book is printed on acid-free paper.

ISBN: 979-8-8230-3445-6 (sc)
ISBN: 979-8-8230-3447-0 (hc)
ISBN: 979-8-8230-3446-3 (e)

Library of Congress Control Number: 2024920605

Print information available on the last page.

Published by AuthorHouse 09/27/2024

authorHOUSE®

Henry the Reading Dog is based on a true story….almost. Jerry is a family friend who introduced his dog Henry, the Irish Setter, to the Reading dog program in Flagstaff Arizona, Paws to Read from 2006-2012. Henry traveled to schools helping children become confident readers by them reading aloud to him. Reading to a dog, the young students feel less nervous or anxious about making mistakes, allowing them to grow into self-confident readers.

Henry the Reading Dog

Henry is an Irish Setter that finds out that being a show dog doesn't make him feel special. One day Henry comes downstairs to find his person, Jerry, reading a book to his granddaughters, Rachel and Brooke.

Henry discovers his love for books and being read to. Brooke is a little girl with beautiful red hair just like Henry. She feels anxious and distressed when reading out loud.

Henry sets off on his quest to find someone to read to him.

It leads him to Brooke's school where he wanders in through an open door to the library. Henry sees Brooke struggling during her turn to read out loud to the class. Brooke and Henry help each other and Henry becomes her school's very first Reading Dog.

Henry, the Irish Setter, grew up in a large family of show dogs. His mother and father were Best in Breed and his Grandfather "Big Red," had earned the title of Best in Show. This meant that Henry's special purpose was being a show dog. Henry had the beautiful coat, the typical Irish Setter build, and the illustrious bloodline. But, Henry did not feel special. He tried to feel unique, but it eluded him.

Despite his family's status akin to royalty in the dog breed world, Henry was unhappy. Being a show dog didn't feel like his true purpose. He believed a special purpose was something felt deep in one's heart, something that allowed one to help others and feel distinct. Something that made you feel, well, special. But Henry just didn't feel special.

Henry sensed he had a special purpose, but what could it be? As Henry underwent his first year of show dog training, he accumulated ribbon after ribbon, much to everyone's delight—except his own. Around his first birthday, seven in dog years, Henry's person sat him down. "Henry," she said, "You seem unenthusiastic. You're not perking your ears up and joyfully running in circles and wagging your tail. I'm not sure being a show dog is your special purpose."

Henry sat down, recalling something his Grandfather had told him. "Someday, you'll feel something that makes your heart happy, causing your ears to perk up, prompting you to run in a circle and let out a happy bark. That will be your special purpose." Henry adored his Grandfather, the most intelligent dog in his pedigree. He respected him deeply, but what did his words mean?

One day, Henry's person summoned him into the living room. "Henry," she said, "This is Jerry." Jerry stood tall with an intelligent smile, casting a happy expression. "Henry, Jerry is your new person," she explained. Henry sat down, bewildered. "New person?" he thought. It was a new experience, and it made his heart race, inducing anxiety.

Soon, Henry found himself being loaded into Jerry's car, and with a click of the car key, they were driving away from everything Henry had ever known—his mother, father, sisters, brothers, and his home. Henry felt scared. In about an hour, Jerry pulled into his driveway in Flagstaff. "Come on, Henry," he said, "This is your new home." Henry felt uncomfortable; now, he had a new person and a new home. He was convinced he'd never discover his special purpose here.

Henry was sad.

The next day, Jerry woke up with the sun. "You are a special boy," Jerry said to Henry. Henry lifted one of his ears to listen to Jerry. "Special." That was a word Grandfather had said to him countless times. "What did that exactly mean?" Henry walked over to Jerry, who patted him on the head and smiled.

Henry, you are part of my family now," Jerry said. Henry looked up at Jerry. He didn't feel special or like a part of Jerry's family.

Every night, when Henry lay down to sleep, he would close his eyes and try to think about what his special purpose was.

Every morning, Jerry would take Henry for a walk to the park through a field of wildflowers.

The scent of the wildflowers always reminded him of his home with his mother and father. Henry would close his eyes and inhale the fragrance of honey and chamomile. It made him happy to smell the sweet scent of flowers and hear the bees going about their day collecting pollen.

Henry loved listening to the bees. He listened to the coyotes howling as they passed through the forest outside their fence. He listened to the baseball games being played at the local field a few streets away, and he listened to Old Mr. and Mrs Jones, who lived next door, as they laughed and reminisced about old stories from their youth.

Listening was something Henry loved to do; it made him happy.

One day Jerry decided to play catch with Henry at the park. He brought a frisbee and explained that he would throw it and Henry was to run and catch it in his mouth. Henry ran in a little circle; his heart felt happy to play a game with Jerry.

Several times a week they would play catch with the frisbee. Henry felt happy and loved to do it because it made him and Jerry happy.

"I will remember this feeling," Henry thought. "Is this my special purpose?" Henry wasn't sure. Jerry always told Henry that he was special and Henry always tried to understand what that meant.

Henry knew his special purpose was out there, and quite possibly, it would be with Jerry.

One morning, Henry woke up and went downstairs. Jerry, his owner, was sitting in the living room with his granddaughters Rachel and Brooke. Rachel had long blonde hair pulled back in a ponytail, and Brooke had long red hair that she often ran her fingers through.

Today Henry noticed that instead of running around making noise and messes, Rachel and Brooke were sitting very quietly on the floor in front of Jerry. Henry could see Jerry holding a book. "Good morning!" Jerry said to Henry. "We are about to read a book. Why don't you join us?"

Henry gladly walked over and found the perfect spot right next to Brooke, where he could put his head in her lap and smell her lovely long hair as she ran her fingers through it. The scent reminded him of the big field in his neighborhood full of wildflowers.

Henry was excited to see Brooke and Rachel, but he was even more excited to find out what reading a book was all about. Once Henry was settled in Brooke's lap, Jerry turned the book to show the girls and Henry the cover and read aloud the title," Puppies Learn a Lesson."

It was a book about a dog and her puppies. Henry's ears perked up. He liked puppies, so he sat perfectly still and listened carefully as Jerry began to read. With every turn of the page, the puppies got into trouble and learned about good manners. Henry felt like he was right there with them on the adventures.

Henry loved listening to Jerry read. Before long, Jerry closed the book and said, "The End." Henry did not want the book to end. He wanted to hear more about the puppies, but Jerry said it was time to go to the park.

Jerry, Brooke, Rachel, and Henry all climbed into the car and drove to the park by the field of flowers. When they arrived, Henry noticed a lady sitting on a park bench. In her hands was what looked like another book. Henry ran to the lady and sat beside her. He perked his ears up when the lady said, "Hello there. Do you want me to read to you?"

Henry wagged his tail as the nice lady began to read the book to him. It was a book about a pirate and a big ship that carried treasure. Henry could almost smell the salt air as she described the ocean, and just as the lady was getting to the part where they buried the treasure, Jerry called Henry. It was time to go home. Henry said goodbye to the nice lady with the book and went home. Henry was sad. He wanted to listen to more books.

The next day, Henry decided to go and look for someone who could read to him. "I know," Henry thought to himself. "I will go and find Jake and Tray." Jake and Tray were twin brothers who lived down the street from Henry and Jerry. Henry remembered he always saw them carrying books when they got off the big yellow school bus.

Henry walked to the street corner where the boys were usually dropped off from school and he waited. Soon, he could see the big yellow school bus turning onto the street. It came to a stop right in front of him.
Jake and Tray stepped out.

Henry was thrilled to see Jake and Tray, and just as he remembered, they were carrying books. "Hi, Henry," they said. "We can't play right now. We have to go home and do homework," Tray said. Henry wagged his tail. "We have to read a book. We have a book report due this week," Tray explained. Henry began jumping with excitement, wagging his tail, and running in a circle.

"Look Jake, Henry wants us to read the book to him," Tray observed. Henry let out a happy bark and followed the boys back to their house. After grabbing a snack, Jake and Tray went outside to sit under the shady apple tree in their backyard. Henry followed them. The boys took turns reading their book out loud. Henry was very happy. The book was about a secret garden in a magical land.

Henry met the school bus every day and followed the boys home to listen to them read. When they finished the book Henry was sad. He wanted to listen to more books but where could he find someone to read to him? Henry walked through town searching the coffee shop, the ice cream parlor and the movie theater. He couldn't find anyone with a book. Suddenly, he remembered Rachel and Brooke. Rachel and Brooke attended a school just a few blocks away. Henry decided to go to Rachel and Brooke's school.

Passing the big field of wildflowers, the duck pond, and Jake and Tray's street, he arrived at the school. He walked through a door and saw a group of children sitting in a circle on the floor in a room filled with walls of books! Henry was happy. He sat in the back with his ears perked up as each of the children took turns reading out loud. The book was about two brothers and a treehouse. Henry enjoyed listening to it. Suddenly, the reading stopped. A little girl with red hair, just like his, sat there with tears rolling down her cheek. Henry recognized the familiar smell—it was Jerry's granddaughter, Brooke.

It was Brooke's turn to read, but she struggled to speak. The kids began to laugh and Brooke started crying. "Why can't she read," asked Kelly. "Maybe she needs glasses," suggested Corbyn. Henry disliked the unkind remarks so he walked over to Brooke, sat next to her, and nuzzled the book with his nose. "Read to me, Brooke," he thought, looking into her crystal blue eyes. Brooke stared at him, and when he nudged the book again, the children fell silent. "He wants you to read to him," the librarian said.

Brooke looked at the book, then back at Henry. He nodded his head and wagged his tail. Brooke took a deep breath and thought of reading to just Henry. She began to feel brave. Henry gave her courage. With Henry's head in her lap, she started to read, initially quietly but gaining confidence as she read aloud, the children began cheering, praising her reading. "Good job," Carly said. "That was great," Sarah chimed in. Brooke felt proud; she was reading to Henry, unafraid. Henry wagged his tail and gave Brooke a big wet lick on her cheek.

"Thank you," Brooke said to Henry. "Will you come again tomorrow for reading in the library?" she asked. Henry ran in a circle, wagging his tail, letting out a happy bark. He knew he didn't have to search for books or people anymore. He would come back to the library and sit with Brooke during reading time. She would be brave and he would be happy listening to her read.

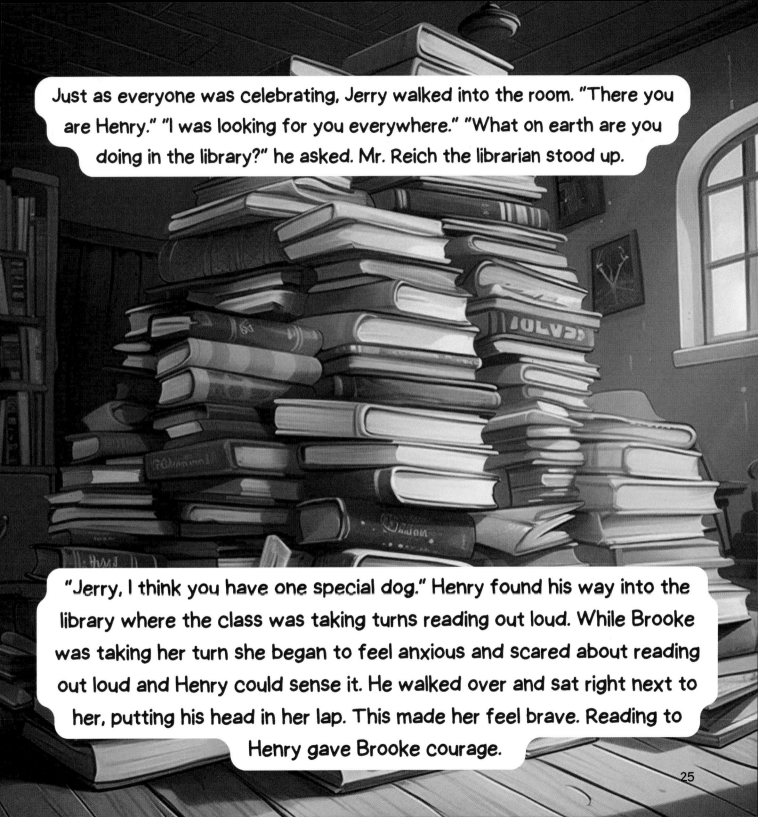

Just as everyone was celebrating, Jerry walked into the room. "There you are Henry." "I was looking for you everywhere." "What on earth are you doing in the library?" he asked. Mr. Reich the librarian stood up.

"Jerry, I think you have one special dog." Henry found his way into the library where the class was taking turns reading out loud. While Brooke was taking her turn she began to feel anxious and scared about reading out loud and Henry could sense it. He walked over and sat right next to her, putting his head in her lap. This made her feel brave. Reading to Henry gave Brooke courage.

"We would like to invite Henry to join us for reading in the library every week," Mr. Reich said to Jerry. All the kids cheered. Jerry smiled. "Well Henry, it looks like we need to get you registered so you can come back to school and listen to the children read books." Henry perked his ears up, ran in a circle and let out a happy bark. Henry felt sure he had finally found his special purpose.

Once Henry was registered, Jerry would drop him off at the library every week. He would sit and listen to the children take turns reading aloud.

Mrs. Penny, Brooke's teacher, noticed that the childrens' reading improved immensely as a result of Henry reading in the library with them. She even had to start a list of names, allowing her to keep track of whose turn it was to sit with Henry. The class loved Henry and Henry loved the class. At the end of the school year, Mrs. Penny and Mr. Reich presented Henry with a medal. It was for being a good citizen and for being the best listener in class. After Henry was given the award, everyone sat together for a class picture, including Henry who was seated right next to Brooke.

He knew he found his special purpose.

This book is dedicated to: Henry and Jerry, my husband Tevis, my children, Teake, Trace, Rachel, Brooke, Cole and my dear friend Krista.
You inspire me to set goals and never forget that everyone has something to offer in life.
This book is also dedicated to Krista's niece, Megan, my daughter Brooke's childhood best friend, who tragically passed away on 07/07/2007 at the age of 7 due to carbon monoxide poisoning while swimming behind an idling ski boat.
Megan loved to read books and she loved animals.
A portion of the proceeds will go to www.meganscause.org as well as to the Flagstaff Paws to Read program in memory of Henry.
If you are interested in finding a reading dog or know of someone who is here is a link to many programs located throughout the United States.
www.pawstoread.com/read-aloud-programs

Henry and Jerry

Printed in the United States
by Baker & Taylor Publisher Services